The Magic Paintbrush

First published in the UK by HarperCollins Children's Books in 2010

1 3 5 7 9 10 8 6 4 2
ISBN: 978-0-00-735573-0

Printed and bound in China

The Magic Paintbrush

HarperCollins *Children's Books*

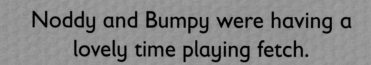

Noddy and Bumpy were having a
lovely time playing fetch.

"Ready, Bumpy?" Noddy asked, as he threw
a stick into the air. "You'll love this one!"

"Woof, woof!" agreed Bumpy.

Suddenly there was a

big bang.

The stick had hit Car and scratched his door!

"Oh, no! I'm sorry, Car," Noddy told his friend.
"Lindy will be able to fix you up. Come on!"

Noddy, Bumpy and Car soon arrived at the garage.

"Hello, Lindy," Noddy said.
"I scratched Car's door and we need to get it fixed."

"A quick lick of yellow paint and you'll be
good as new!" Lindy told Car.

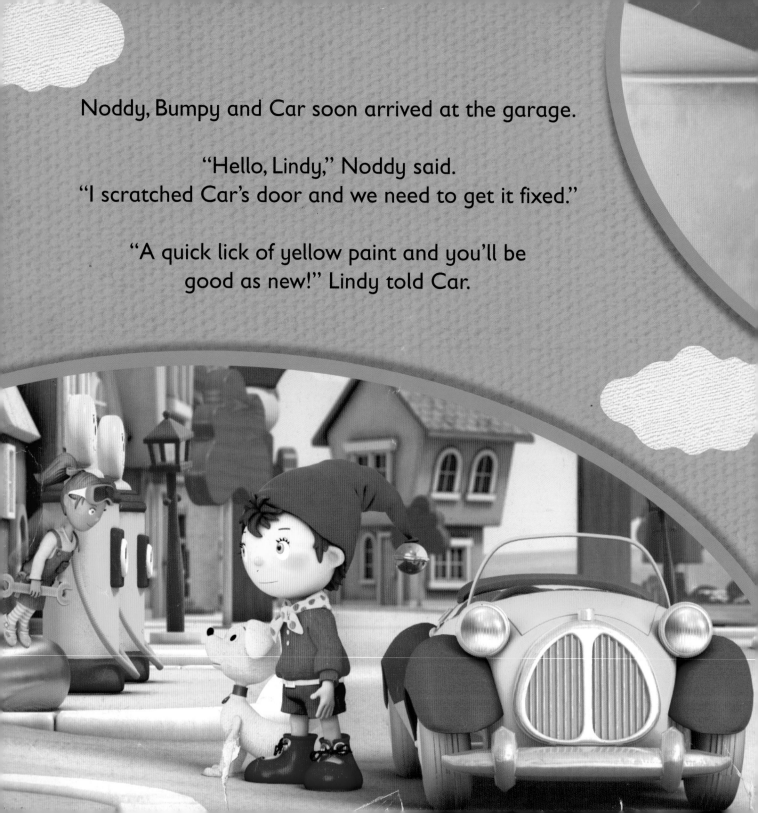

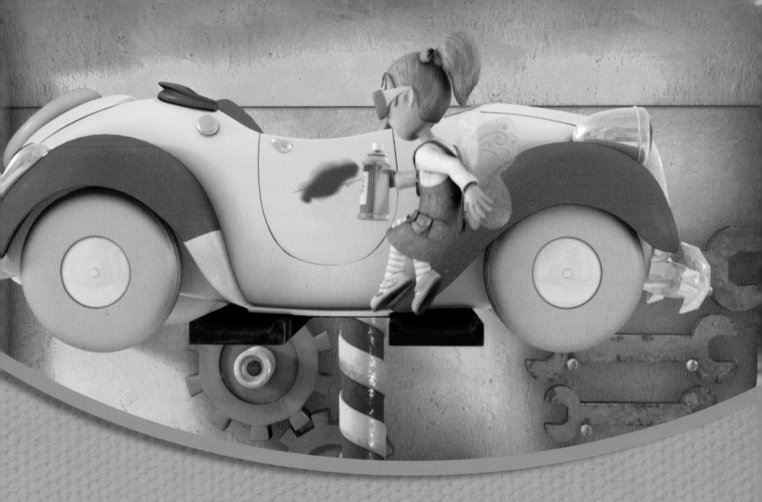

Lindy set to work,
but when she sprayed her yellow paint, it came out purple!

"Oh, no!" she cried. "I must have picked up the wrong can!"

They searched and searched, but they couldn't
find the yellow paint anywhere. Noddy decided to ask
Big Ears for help.

Big Ears was sitting outside the ice cream parlour.

"Look what happened to Car!" said Noddy,
pointing at his friend.

"Oh! Gracious! Poor Car!" cried Big Ears.

Big Ears didn't have any yellow paint but he
did have something else…

"My magic paintbrush! I just need to say some magic words to get it going," Big Ears told Noddy.

"Magic paintbrush, clever fellow, Noddy needs you and your yellow!"

The magic paintbrush sparkled
and turned yellow!

"Yes! It works!"

said Noddy, as he painted over the
scratch on Car's door.

"Down, Bumpy!"
laughed Noddy as Bumpy
tried to grab the magic paintbrush.
"This isn't a stick, you know!"

"Woof! Woof!"

barked Bumpy, excitedly.

Noddy and Big Ears decided to have some
tea and cakes. Noddy left the magic paintbrush
outside the ice cream parlour.

"Mmmm! Yum! Lovely!"

said Noddy, as he tucked into a scrummy muffin.

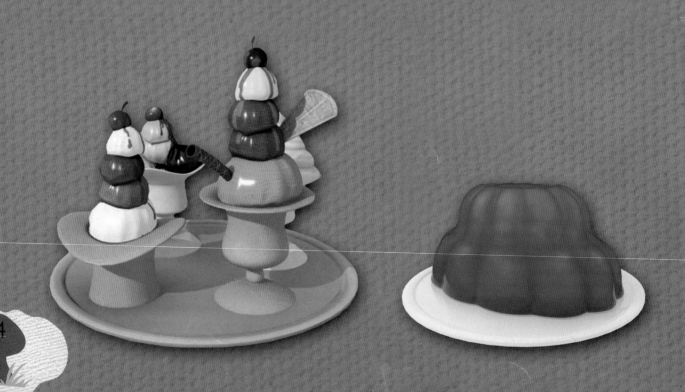

Suddenly Car started beeping outside.

"Something must be wrong!"
cried Noddy, rushing out of the door.

Noddy couldn't believe his eyes…
Car was covered in green spots!

"The magic paintbrush has gone wild!"
shouted Noddy. "We've got to find it
before it does any more damage!"

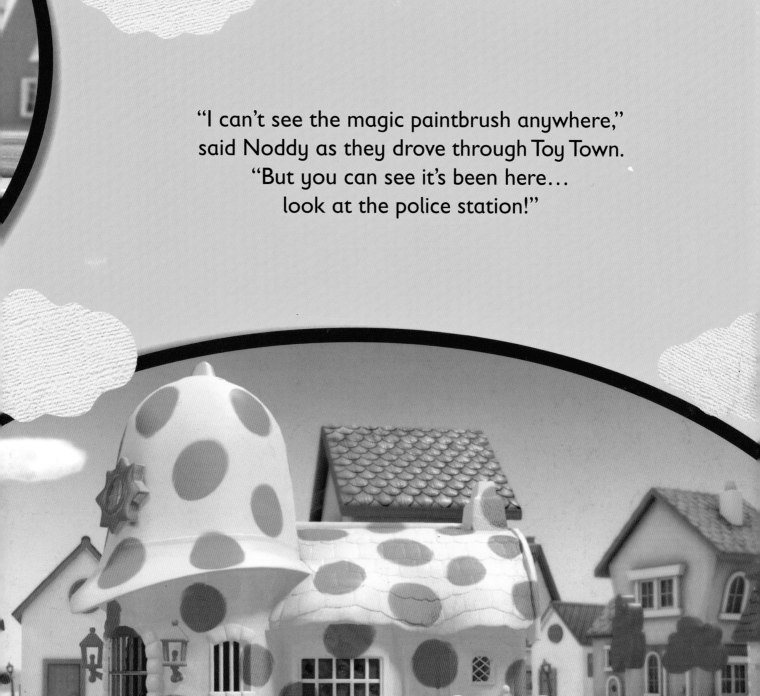

"I can't see the magic paintbrush anywhere,"
said Noddy as they drove through Toy Town.
"But you can see it's been here...
look at the police station!"

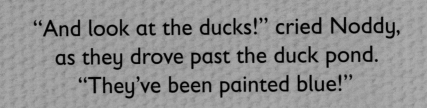

"And look at the ducks!" cried Noddy,
as they drove past the duck pond.
"They've been painted blue!"

"Quack, Quack!"

said the blue ducks.

Even Mr Wobbly Man had been painted! He looked very
funny with a big red stripe down his front!

"We need to find Mr Plod," said Mr Wobbly Man,
as he wobbled down the street.

Wobble, wobble, wobble!

19

As Noddy drove through Toy Town, he saw that more and more things had been painted.

The trees were purple, the town hall clock was covered in spots and the little skittles had silly faces!

"Ha, ha, ha!"

chuckled the little skittles as they looked at each other.

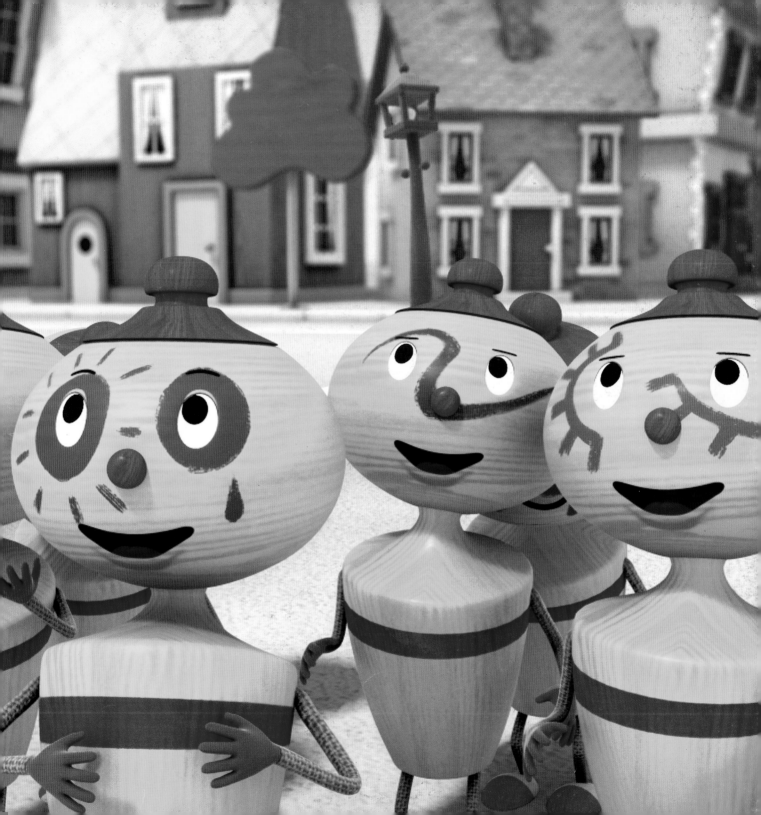

Just then, Mr Plod arrived.
"What's been going on here?" he asked.

"My magic paintbrush is making trouble and I
can't think how to stop it," Big Ears told him.
"I must go and fetch my magic book."

That gave Noddy an idea!

"Fetch! Of course! That's it!" he cried, as he got out of Car.
"Bumpy loves playing fetch. He can fetch the Magic Paintbrush!"

Big Ears and Tessie thought that was a great idea.

23

"Fetch,
Bumpy,
fetch!"

Noddy shouted.

24

Bumpy chased the magic paintbrush
and jumped as high as he could.
Everyone cheered as he caught the
paintbrush in his mouth!

"Well done, Noddy and Bumpy!" praised Mr Plod.
"Now we need to put Toy Town back the way it was."

"Shall we use magic?" asked Tessie.

"We don't need any more magic!" laughed Noddy.
"Let's repaint Toy Town together. It'll be fun!"

Everyone worked as hard as they could.
Soon Toy Town looked as good as new.

"That's much better!"

said Mrs Skittle,
as she painted the last duck yellow.

There was a special treat
waiting for everyone when they
finished…lots of yummy cupcakes!

"Here you are, Bumpy,"
said Noddy, offering his
friend a cake. "Fetch!"

"Woof! Woof!"

barked Bumpy, happily.

NODDY
IN TOYLAND®

Look out for more
Noddy in Toyland books!

The Magic Watering Can

Noddy and the Pirate

Hide-and-Seek Fun

A Very Special Birthday

Noddy Goes Vroom!

See Noddy's new vehicles inside!